**W9-CPW-063**

# SAYINGS and PHRASES

# I'm All Thumbs!

## (And Other Odd Things We Say)

written by Cynthia Amoroso ★ illustrated by Mernie Gallagher-Cole

## ABOUT THE AUTHOR

As a high school English teacher and as an elementary teacher, Cynthia Amoroso has shared her love of language with students. She has always been fascinated with idioms and figures of speech. Today Cynthia is a school district administrator in Minnesota. She has two daughters who also share her love of language through reading, writing, and talking!

## ABOUT THE ILLUSTRATOR

Mernie Gallagher-Cole lives in Pennsylvania with her husband and two children. She uses sayings and phrases like the ones in this book every day. She has illustrated many children's books, including *Messy Molly* and *Día De Los Muertos* for The Child's World®.

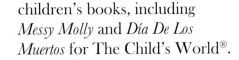

# The Child's World®

Published by The Child's World®
1980 Lookout Drive • Mankato, MN 56003-1705
800-599-READ • www.childsworld.com

**ACKNOWLEDGMENTS**
The Child's World®: Mary Berendes,
Publishing Director

The Design Lab: Kathleen Petelinsek,
Design and Page Production

**LIBRARY OF CONGRESS CATALOGING-IN-PUBLICATION DATA**
Amoroso, Cynthia.
 I'm all thumbs!: (and other odd things we say) / by Cynthia Amoroso; Illustrated by Mernie Gallagher-Cole.
   p. cm.
 ISBN 978-1-60253-682-1 (library bound: alk. paper)
 1. English language—Idioms—Juvenile literature.
 2. Figures of speech—Juvenile literature. 3. Clichés—Juvenile literature. I. Gallagher-Cole, Mernie. II. Title.
 PE1460.A584 2011
 428.1—dc22                              2010042739

Printed in the United States of America
Mankato, MN
December, 2010
PA02067

*People use idioms (ID-ee-umz) every day. These are sayings and phrases with meanings that are different from the actual words. Some idioms seem silly. Many of them don't make much sense . . . at first.*

*This book will help you understand some of the most common idioms. It will tell you how you might hear a saying or phrase. It will tell you what the saying really means. All of these sayings and short phrases—even the silly ones—are an important part of our language!*

# TABLE of CONTENTS

# At the drop of a hat

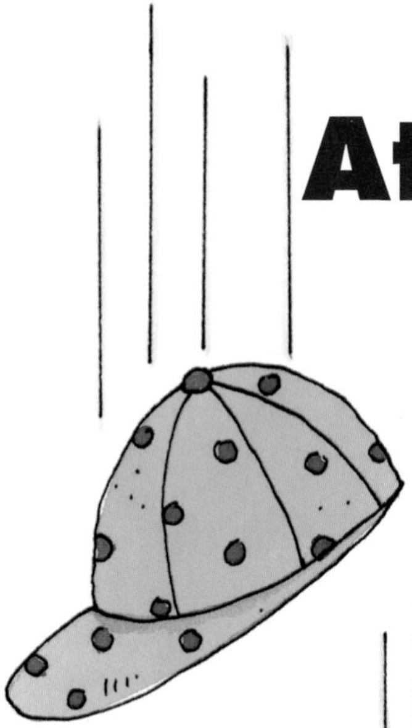

Mom walked into the house and hung up her coat.

"How did it go?" asked Dad.

"Fine!" said Mom. "Anna signed up for soccer, and Eric signed up for baseball."

"Baseball?" asked Dad. "This morning he said he wanted to take karate. That boy changes his mind at the drop of a hat!"

**MEANING: To do something quickly; to make a decision quickly, sometimes for no reason**

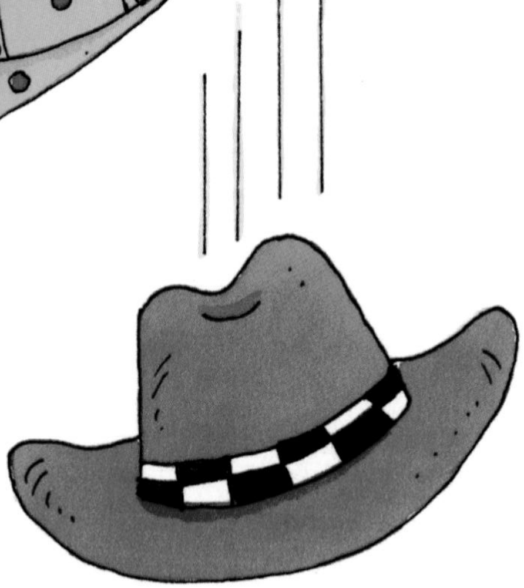

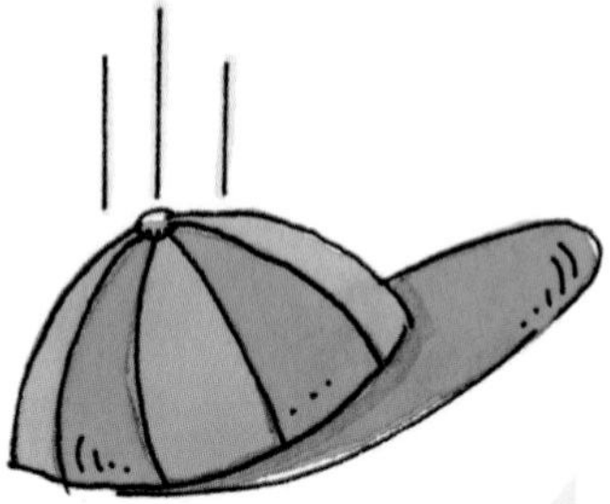

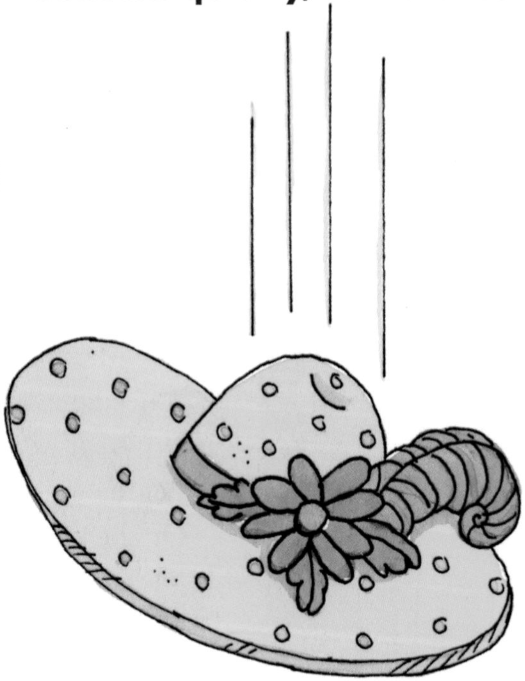

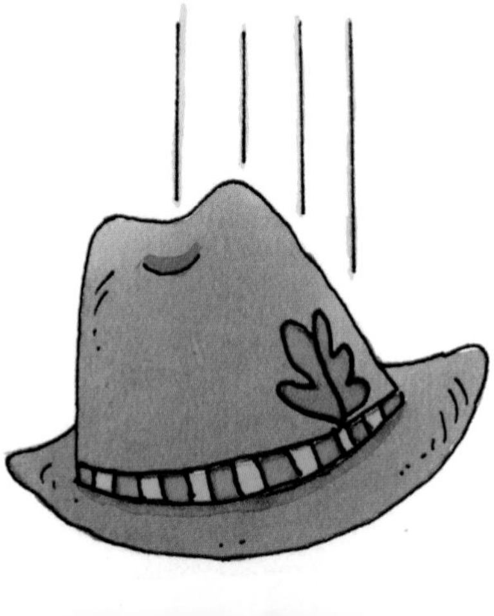

# The big cheese

Noah had just been elected class president. Teachers and students had been congratulating him all day. He couldn't wait to tell his parents when he got home.

"Congratulations!" said Mom when Noah told her about his big day. "So, how does it feel to be the big cheese?"

"It feels great!" answered Noah.

**MEANING: To be important; to be in charge; to get attention**

# A bird's eye view

Eve's family was excited to visit Chicago. Today they were at the top of the Willis Tower.

"I can look down on those clouds from above!" gasped her sister.

"Look over here," said Eve. "You can see for miles!"

"This is amazing," Dad agreed. "It certainly is a bird's eye view."

**MEANING: To see things from up high**

# By the book

Cooper's family was going to spend the weekend at Uncle Jon's campground.

"Let's go straight to number five!" Cooper said. "That's the best camping spot."

"Hold on," said Dad. "We have to go to the office first."

"Why?" asked Cooper. "Uncle Jon knows who we are."

"We still have to fill out a form, just like everybody else," Dad said. "Uncle Jon does things by the book."

**MEANING: To do something strictly by the rules; to follow directions or guidelines closely**

# A clean slate

Isabella's soccer team ended the season on a bad note. They lost some important games, and their best three players moved away. Now it was time to start practicing again.

"I know you're all unhappy about last season," said the coach. "But let's forget about that. This is a new beginning. We're starting with a clean slate."

**MEANING: A new start, made possible by erasing what came before**

# The cream of the crop

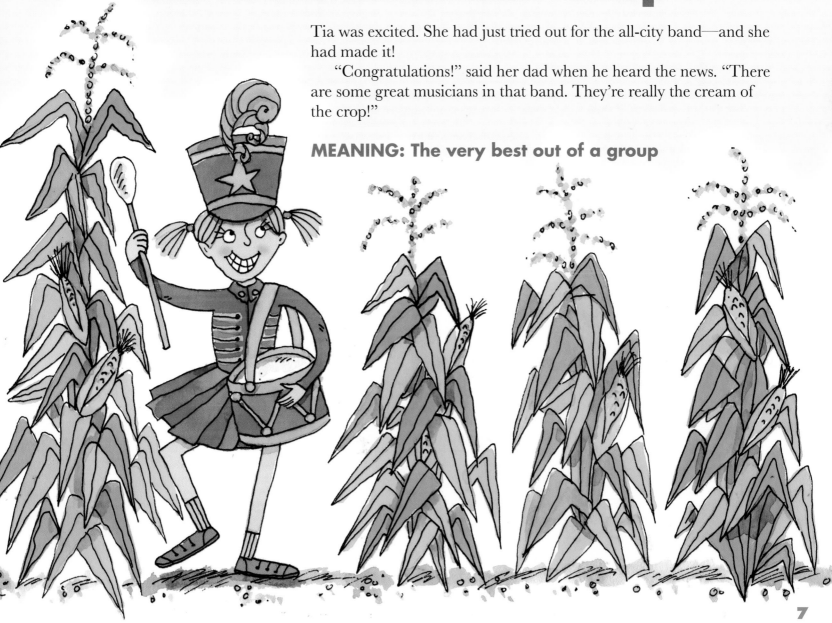

Tia was excited. She had just tried out for the all-city band—and she had made it!

"Congratulations!" said her dad when he heard the news. "There are some great musicians in that band. They're really the cream of the crop!"

**MEANING: The very best out of a group**

# Don't rock the boat

Jared and his classmates had written a play for their drama class. They were going to perform it at a school assembly tomorrow.

"I think we should redo the ending," Jared said suddenly. He explained his idea.

"It's a fun idea," said Mr. Harter, the drama teacher, "but it's a big change! You're all ready for the assembly tomorrow. You can always change the ending later, but for now—don't rock the boat!"

**MEANING: To upset a stable situation; to upset something that's going well**

# Easy come, easy go

Tony knocked on his sister's bedroom door.

"Hey, Amy," said Tony, "may I borrow five dollars?"

"Didn't you just get paid for mowing the Smiths' lawn?" asked Amy.

"I already spent that," said Tony. "I'll pay you back tomorrow when I mow the Wilsons' lawn."

"I can't believe how fast you spend your money," Amy said. "It's just easy come, easy go."

**MEANING: To get something quickly or easily and then lose it or spend it quickly**

# Flip your lid

Stacy was really mad. Her brother Ethan had gotten into her art supplies. Now she couldn't find the glue she needed to finish her school project.

"Ethan!" Stacy shouted. "You made a mess in here. Now I can't find anything! "

"Okay, okay," said Ethan. "Don't flip your lid!"

**MEANING: To get angry; to lose control**

9

# For what it's worth

Sofia was feeling sad. She had been really nice to Mandy. Now Mandy was having a party, but she hadn't invited Sofia.

"I know you feel unhappy about this," Dad said. "For what it's worth, I don't think Mandy has been a very good friend to you. This might be a chance to learn about what makes a good friendship."

**MEANING: To give advice or your opinion even if it is not important, or even though the other person might not ask for it**

# Get off on the wrong foot

Mom walked in the door, put down her bag, and flopped down on the couch.

"Hey, Mom," said Nick. "Are you okay?"

"I'm just tired," replied Mom. "It's been a long week."

"Is your new boss still causing problems?" asked Nick.

"Not really. You know, she's actually turning out okay. I think we just got off on the wrong foot. "

**MEANING: To have trouble getting along with someone you've just met**

Wrong

Right

# Get your second wind

Jake had been at football camp all afternoon. The weather was hot, and he was tired. Finally the coach called a break. The whole team had something to drink and sat in the shade. Then the coach blew his whistle and hollered, "Everybody up!"

"Had enough?" whispered Jake's older brother.

"No," Jake replied. "That break was all I needed. Now I have my second wind."

**MEANING: To get energy or feel wide awake after feeling tired or sleepy**

# Half the battle

Diego and his family were on their way home from vacation. It had been a terrible morning! The rental car had a flat tire. Then Dad took a wrong turn on the highway. They barely made it to the airport in time.

"Whew," sighed Dad as they reached their plane's gate. "We made it! Just getting to the plane was half the battle. Now let's hope the flight goes smoothly, and we get all our luggage when we land!"

**MEANING: A successful start to something that takes time or energy**

# Head in the clouds

Krista had a great imagination. She loved to daydream about places she would love to go and things she would like to do. But sometimes she didn't pay much attention to the things around her. Today, she was supposed to be helping Grandma weed her garden. Instead, she was dragging her fingers through the dirt, dreaming of faraway lands.

"Krista!" called Grandma. "You really have your head in the clouds! I have a whole bucket full of weeds, and you don't even have one."

**MEANING: Lost in thought; absentminded**

# Hot off the press

Beth had spent all afternoon in her room. Finally, she sat down to supper with her family.

"Goodness, you look tired. What have you doing up there?" asked Mom.

"I've been making a flyer for getting babysitting jobs," said Beth. "I'm going to send copies to all the neighbors." Beth took a flyer from her pocket. "Here's the first one, hot off the press. You're the first person to see it!"

**MEANING: Something has just been finished or completed**

# I'm all thumbs

Ben's art project was due tomorrow. He was trying to decorate a birdhouse using twigs and glue. But no matter what he did, the twigs wouldn't stay where he glued them.

"I give up!" Ben complained to his sister. "I can draw really well, but I just can't do this kind of stuff. When it comes to gluing things, I'm all thumbs!"

**MEANING: To have trouble using your fingers when working with small objects; to feel awkward when doing something with your hands**

# Keep your eyes peeled

Charlie and his Dad were driving around, looking for an ice-cream store Charlie wanted to visit.

"I know it's around here somewhere," said Charlie. "I rode my bike past it on Saturday."

"Okay," said Dad. "Keep your eyes peeled, and let me know when you see it."

**MEANING: To keep a close watch; to look carefully for something**

# The lesser of two evils

Conner was helping his dad clean up. Finally, there were only two jobs left—cleaning the garage and weeding the garden.

"Those are both terrible jobs!" said Conner.

"I know," said Dad with a smile. "Let's split them up. You pick one, and I'll do the other one."

"I'll weed the garden," said Conner. "It's the lesser of two evils."

**MEANING: A choice that isn't quite as bad as the other one**

# My lips are sealed

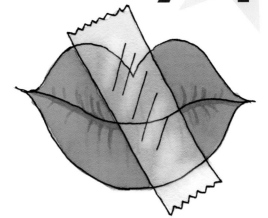

The party for Lily's dad was in three days. Lily thought of a special surprise. She ran downstairs to tell her mom.

She whispered her idea, and her mom smiled with delight.

"But don't tell Dad!" said Lily. "I want him to be surprised!"

"Don't worry. My lips are sealed," Mom promised.

**MEANING: A promise to keep a secret**

# The Midas touch

Audrey and her family were driving to Uncle Ryan's house. Audrey loved visiting Uncle Ryan. She always had fun with him.

"Dad, what does Uncle Ryan do for his job?" asked Audrey.

"He invents things," said Dad. "He's very smart, and he has lots of great ideas. He's sold a bunch of his ideas to big companies, for lots of money. You could say he has the Midas touch!"

**MEANING: Able to make a lot of money; successful at whatever you do**

# A needle in a haystack

Sara and her family were camping. Suddenly she realized she had lost her favorite necklace. It was bright green, and the grass and leaves were bright green, too.

"Mom," she pleaded, "how will we ever find it?"

"I don't know!" said Mom. "I wish it were a different color. Finding that necklace out here is like finding a needle in a haystack."

**MEANING: Something that seems impossible to find**

# No sweat

Lucas was trying to move his basketball hoop a little lower. He could reach it, but he couldn't get it to move. Finally he saw his big brother coming.

"Hey, Michael!" he shouted. "Can you help me move this thing? It's stuck again."

"No sweat," Michael answered. "I'll be right there."

**MEANING: To do something easily; to not be worried about something**

# Off the wall

Oliver was reading a new book. His best friend had recommended it.

"Do you like it?" asked Ms. Valdez, the school librarian.

Oliver stopped to think. "Well, the characters are really weird. And the story goes all over the place. In fact, it's really off the wall! But it's pretty funny."

**MEANING: When something is very different and seems strange**

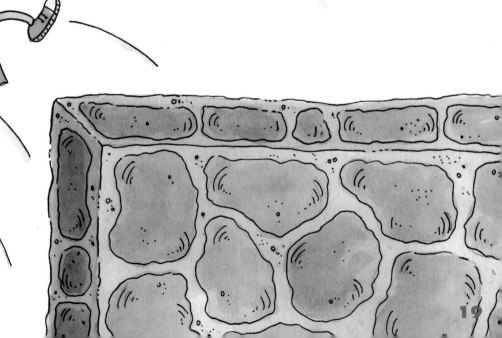

# On the up-and-up

Aiden was looking for a summer job. "Hey, Dad!" he hollered. "I might have found something!"

He handed his dad a clipping out of the local newspaper.

"Hmmm," said his dad. "This sounds a little too good to be true. Let's look into it first. We want to make sure everything is on the up-and-up."

**MEANING: Honest**

# Packed in like sardines

Cameron and his sisters were on their way to a tennis match. All three were wedged into the backseat of a small car, holding their bags.

"I'm squished!" complained Cameron.

Mom said, "Sorry, kids! The van wasn't running properly this morning, so I had to borrow Grandma's car. I know you're packed in like sardines, but we're almost there."

**MEANING: Very crowded**

# Pull the rug out from under you

Sadie was upset. She'd been planning to stay at her friend Nora's this weekend. But her mom had just announced they were going to Aunt Sue's instead.

"But Mom," Sadie protested. "We've been planning this for days!"

"I know," said Mom. "I'm sorry to pull the rug out from under you, but this is important. Aunt Sue needs our help."

**MEANING: When someone does something to upset your plans**

# Put your money where your mouth is

Isaac had been practicing his free throws for weeks. Now he was ready to take on his older cousin Ryan. "Come on, Ryan," Isaac teased. "I bet I can beat you. Let's see who's best."

"We already know who's best," said Ryan with a grin.

"Yeah," said Isaac, "and it's me!"

"Oh, yeah?" said Ryan, tossing the ball to him. "Okay, kid, put your money where your mouth is! Let's see what you can do."

**MEANING: A challenge to prove that you can do something you say you can do**

# Run-of-the-mill

Charlotte was waiting for her cousins to arrive. They had spent the day at the new water park. Charlotte was eager to hear all about it.

"It was okay," cousin Elijah said when he arrived.

"Just okay?" Charlotte asked.

"Just okay," repeated Uncle Dave. "Compared to other water parks, this one was pretty run-of-the-mill."

**MEANING: Average or nothing special; ordinary**

# Short and sweet

Andrew's baseball team had just come from a tournament. They'd played in the hot sun and ridden on the bus for hours. But they still needed to find out about next week's practices.

"All right," said the coach. "I know you're all tired, and you want to go home. So we'll make this short and sweet. I'll just give you the basics now and then e-mail you the details."

**MEANING: Done quickly or briefly; done without wasting any time**

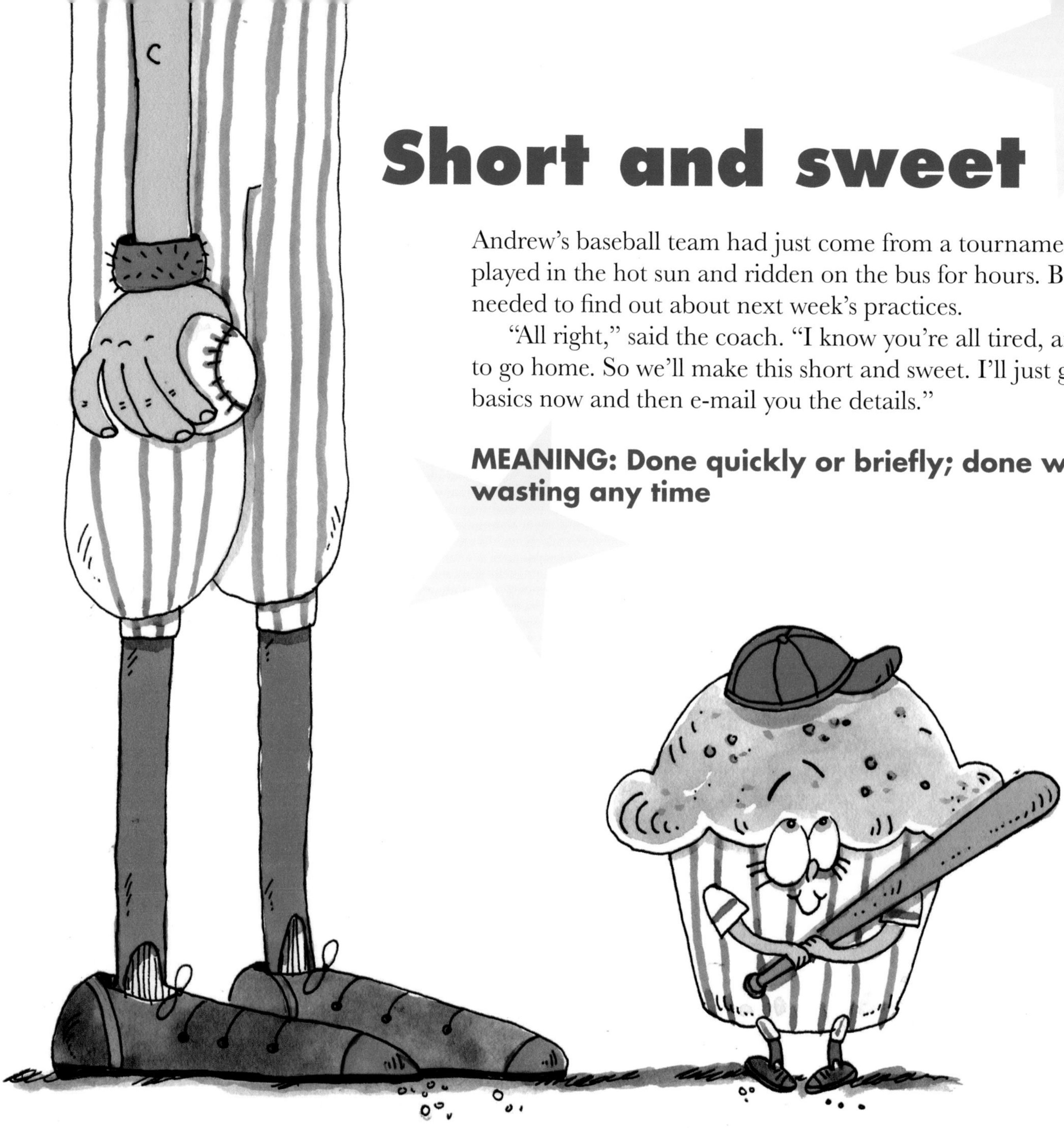